Pageant

Book and Lyrics by
Bill Russell and Frank Kelly

Music by
Albert Evans

Conceived by
Robert Longbottom

A SAMUEL FRENCH ACTING EDITION

SAMUEL
FRENCH
FOUNDED 1830

SAMUELFRENCH.COM
SAMUELFRENCH-LONDON.CO.UK

FOR PRODUCTION ENQUIRIES

UNITED STATES AND CANADA
Info@SamuelFrench.com
1-866-598-8449

UNITED KINGDOM AND EUROPE
Plays@SamuelFrench-London.co.uk
020-7255-4302

Each title is subject to availability from Samuel French, depending upon
country of performance. Please be aware that *PAGEANT* may not be
licensed by Samuel French in your territory. Professional and amateur
producers should contact the nearest Samuel French office or licensing
partner to verify availability.

RENTAL MATERIALS

An orchestration consisting of **Piano/Conductor Score, Synthesizer, Guitar, Bass, Drums, Miss West Coast Dance CD, and 6 Chorus Books** will be loaned two months prior to the production ONLY on the receipt of the Licensing Fee quoted for all performances, the rental fee and a refundable deposit. Please contact Samuel French for perusal of the music materials as well as a performance license application.

MUSIC USE NOTE

Licensees are solely responsible for obtaining formal written permission from copyright owners to use copyrighted music in the performance of this play and are strongly cautioned to do so. If no such permission is obtained by the licensee, then the licensee must use only original music that the licensee owns and controls. Licensees are solely responsible and liable for all music clearances and shall indemnify the copyright owners of the play(s) and their licensing agent, Samuel French, against any costs, expenses, losses and liabilities arising from the use of music by licensees. Please contact the appropriate music licensing authority in your territory for the rights to any incidental music.

IMPORTANT BILLING AND CREDIT REQUIREMENTS

If you have obtained performance rights to this title, please refer to your licensing agreement for important billing and credit requirements.

PAGEANT, book and lyrics by Bill Russell and Frank Kelly, music by Albert Evans, orchestrations, musical arrangements and musical direction by James Raitt, sets by Daniel Ettinger, costume design by Gregg Barnes, lighting by Timothy Hunter, hair design by Lazaro Arencibia, production stage manager Debora Porazzi, casting by Joseph Abaldo, co-choreographer Tony Parise, conceived, directed and choreographed by Robert Longbottom, presented by Jonathan Scharer in association with Chip Quigley, opened at the Blue Angel, May 2, 1991 with the following cast and musicians:

THE CAST

MISS BIBLE BELT	Randl Ask
MISS DEEP SOUTH	David Drake
MISS TEXAS	Russell Garrett
MISS INDUSTRIAL NORTHEAST	Joe Joyce
MISS WEST COAST	John Salvatore
MISS GREAT PLAINS	Dick Scanlan
FRANKIE CAVALIER	J.T. Cromwell

Standby Contestant	Jack Plotnick
Standby for Frankie Cavalier	Larry Hansen

MUSICIANS:

Conductor/Piano: JAMES RAITT
Synthesizer Programmer: MARTIN ERSKINE
Drummer: JEFF POTTER

AUTHOR'S NOTE

It is our intent that the contestants in the Miss Glamouresse Pageant be portrayed by men because women wouldn't do it the same way.

ABOUT PAGEANT

PAGEANT is a pageant. Judges selected from the audience actually vote and determine the winner who, therefore, may be different at each performance. The show takes its shots *not* by mocking the pageant from the outside, but by *being one*. The show works best when it sticks to the format and spirit of the pageant. Audiences know a lot more about pageants than they think they do (or than they are willing to admit). A case in point: in the early development of the show there was a big production number about how the contestants had gotten to the semi-finals; it had several self-contained scenes and songs and a rousing choral finale. The audience reaction ranged from mild to hearty approval. But when we took out this sequence and moved more quickly to the more generic elements of the pageant, beyond question the show worked better; it had rediscovered its engine.

About those girls: the more specific the characters, the more particular the actors can make them, the funnier they are. Generalized, stereotyped characterizations (the ditz, the bitch, Ms. Clueless), however amusing for a moment, just don't work over the long haul. A natural focal point for the characters is the contest itself. What did they have to do to get there? What would winning mean to them? How did they get involved in this thing in the first place? The audience may never hear the answers to these questions, but if the *actors* know the answers it invariably shows up in their on-stage performance, in the interview, in the spokesmodel spots, etc. Men in dresses may be funny by itself—for about 5 minutes. Then it's up to the characters. As a reviewer astutely noted, "What makes the show so funny is that these are actors *portraying* women, not actors trying to convince you that they *are* women. The distinction is subtle but it marks the difference between comedy and mere camp." One person wins this contest; everybody else loses, to greater or lesser degrees. Because this pageant is happening on stage, we get to see the losers' reactions in much greater detail than in sanitized TV pageants. This can make the end of the show truly riotous, but only if the stakes for each of the contestants have been clearly set up beforehand. *Pageant* should be played as real as possible. Audiences want to go with the reality of it because that way they can enjoy it as a contest; they develop stakes in the outcome. The wink-wink-nudge-nudge approach may work on a joke by joke basis, but it undermines the event because it denies that something real is going on. And if on some level, *Pageant* isn't real, then it's just not a pageant.

CHARACTER DESCRIPTIONS

All actors need to sing, move well and have strong comedy skills. The actors playing the CONTESTANTS should at the very least look presentable as female beauty pageant contestants. The idea is to present male actors as female characters—not over-the-top drag queens.

MISS BIBLE BELT, RUTH ANN RUTH — believes that she plus God equals a majority in any situation. *Nobody* is better connected than she is. She sees even the cheesiest part of the Glamouresse Beauty Regimen as part of His Plan. This gives her a righteous attitude which is unshakable, but she also has the manic cheerfulness of the newly saved. Big belter voice — strongest singer in cast.

MISS DEEP SOUTH, LAURINDA SUMMERFORD — The Blonde in the show; even though others may have blonde hair, only she knows how to work it. At the same time (and she sees no contradiction in this) she is The Lady, the only one of the contestants (she believes) who knows that in order to be a winner, a lady always has to come in second *to her man.* She has a very narrow and ritualized sense of "femininity" which is frequently outraged by the other contestants' behavior and attitudes. Her talent is ventriloquism, so some vocal dexterity is helpful.

MISS GREAT PLAINS, BONNIE LOUISE CUTLETT — utterly sincere in her belief in the values promoted by Glamouresse, though some of them seem quite exotic to her. She is honored to represent the great heartland of this nation and to show what honest country folk can do. Winning her region was "beyond her wildest dreams." In the present contest she is agape and aglow. Not necessarily the "prettiest" contestant.

MISS INDUSTRIAL NORTHEAST, CONSUELA MANUELA RAFAELLA LOPEZ — included among the regional winners mostly due to Glamouresse's belated sense that, marketing-wise, the times they are a-changin' and to the Northeast's notable lack of interest in the contest. Her talent has been culled from watching, with religious fervor, the variety show "Sabado Gigante" on Spanish television.

Actor must be able at least to stand on roller- or in-line skates and (possibly) be able to create a different character for the reigning Miss Glamouresse.

MISS TEXAS, KITTY-BOB AMES — the Professional of the group. With her father's money and a shrewd selection of contests, she has never lost a competition. Her skills may not be outstanding by themselves, but her attitude says "Winner" all the way. She doesn't so much want to win as she does *expect* to win. Actor must tap dance to some rudimentary extent.

MISS WEST COAST, KARMA QUINN — like Miss Great Plains, is sweet-natured, but Karma is a *lot less focused.* She has tried to parlay her vagueness and I'll-try-anything-once attitude into a comprehensive mystical spirituality but it hasn't jelled. This pageant is the most structured event of her entire life. Karma became a regional winner when the first, second and third place contestants were killed in a freak accident on the Universal Studios Tour. Actor should have some dance skills and (possibly) be able to create a different character for the reigning Miss Glamouresse.

FRANKIE CAVALIER — our genial host, is *certainly* that. He relishes his role of m.c., is proud to be associated with a "prestigious" company such as Glamouresse, and is delighted to find himself the center of attention of so many gorgeous gals. Frankie is a third or fourth-tier celebrity who is known to the audience where the pageant is being performed, perhaps as a weekend weather-report reader or a spokesman for a used car dealership. His contract with the pageant is up for renewal this year. Strong singer who moves well.

PAGEANT

(MUSIC #1 — OVERTURE)

CONTESTANTS. *(Off-Stage.)*
OOH AHHH
MISS GLAMOURESSE
OOH AHHH
SHE'S THE ONE
FRANKIE. *(Off-Stage, Over Overture.)* Ladies and gentlemen, welcome to [Name of Theatre] in beautiful downtown [Name of City], home of the [Upcoming Year] Miss Glamouresse Pageant—featuring the all-natural sound of [Orchestra Conductor] and his Scintillating Synthesizers! The management reminds you that the taking of photographs or the use of recording equipment is hazardous to the performers, distracting to the audience and against the law.

(MUSIC #2 — "NATURAL BORN FEMALES")

CONTESTANTS. *(Off-Stage.)*
WHO WILL IT BE?
FRANKIE. *(Off-Stage.)* Ladies and gentlemen, we are gathered here to answer one all-important question:
CONTESTANTS.
MIRROR, MIRROR OF SUCCESS
WHO WILL BE MISS GLAMOURESSE?
FRANKIE. *(Off-Stage.)* There's only one way to find out! *So let the beauty begin!!!!!*

(The curtain opens to reveal SIX CONTESTANTS who march Downstage singing.)

9

CONTESTANTS.
WE ARE NATURAL BORN FEMALES
AND WE WANT TO SING IT LOUD
WE ARE NATURAL BORN FEMALES
AND WE'RE PROUD, PROUD, PROUD
WE HAVE ALL THE RIGHT EQUIPMENT
BY NATURE WE'RE ENDOWED
IT'S OUR BIRTHRIGHT AND DUTY
TO WORK HARD AT BEAUTY
AND WE'RE PROUD, PROUD, PROUD

WE DON'T NEED TO RAISE OUR VOICES
TO GET OUR POINTS ACROSS
WE DON'T NEED TO SERVE OUR DISHES
STRIPPED OF ALL THEIR SAUCE
WE DON'T HAVE TO BE UNCOUTH
OR UN-AMER-I-CAN
WE DON'T HAVE TO STAY ON TOP
BY ACTING LIKE A MAN

And speaking of men...
MISS GREAT PLAINS. Our Master of Ceremonies...
MISS INDUSTRIAL NORTHEAST. ... is a perfect specimen!
MISS BIBLE BELT. A personal friend of Wayne Newton!
MISS TEXAS. Spokesman for the International Hair Barn for Men!
MISS DEEP SOUTH. The host of t.v.'s runaway hit!
MISS WEST COAST. "America's Goofiest People!"
ALL CONTESTANTS. FRANKIE CAVALIER!!!

(FRANKIE CAVALIER enters, carrying his ever-present, wireless, handheld microphone.)

FRANKIE. Thank you, girls, for that introduction and especially for being your ever-lovin' gorgeous selves.

WHAT A NIGHT! WHAT A NIGHT! WHAT A NIGHT!
BEAUTIES TO THE LEFT OF ME

AND BEAUTIES TO MY RIGHT
THEY TOLD ME NOT TO KISS THE GIRLS
BUT STILL I THINK I MIGHT
WHAT A NIGHT!
WHAT A NIGHT!
WHAT A NIGHT!
    CONTESTANTS.
WE ARE NATURAL BORN FEMALES
AND WE LOVE A NATURAL MAN
    FRANKIE.
CAN YOU HUG HIM AND SQUEEZE HIM?
    CONTESTANTS.
YES WE CAN, CAN, CAN!!!
YOU'RE OUR FAVORITE KIND OF SINGER
AND SUAVE CO-ME-DI-AN
    FRANKIE.
AM I TENDER, YET MACHO?
AND HOT AS A NACHO?
    CONTESTANTS.
YOU'RE OUR FAVORITE MAN!!!

(CONTESTANTS fawn over FRANKIE.)

FRANKIE.	**CONTESTANTS.**
Thank you ... aw, gee, thank you.	OH WHAT A NIGHT
You're my favorite girls and this is	OH WHAT A NIGHT
my favorite night of the year. And as	OH WHAT A NIGHT
I always say:	OH WHAT A NIGHT

The Super Bowl's swell
The Oscars all right
But nothing compares
With Glamouresse night

Because that's when one of the	OH WHAT A NIGHT
country's top purveyors of beauty	OH WHAT A NIGHT
products crowns its queen. Of course	OH WHAT A NIGHT
that company is our own Glamouresse	OH WHAT A NIGHT

FRANKIE. (cont.)
and I am so ... honored that they have
asked me to host this momentous event
for the second year ... in a row! But
enough about me—LET THE BEAUTY
CONTINUE!

CONTESTANTS.
OH WHAT A NIGHT
OH WHAT A NIGHT

CONTESTANTS.
WE DON'T HAVE TO DRESS IN PANTS SUITS
TO PROVE WE RUN THE SHOW
WE DON'T HAVE TO GIVE UP HIGH HEELS
TO PROVE WE'RE ON THE GO
WE DON'T HAVE TO GET A JOB
TO PROVE WE HOLD OUR OWN
AND WE DON'T HAVE TO BE HARD-BOILED
IF WE STAY SOFT AT HOME

FRANKIE.
Our six contestants this evening
became regional winners by undergoing
an exhausting series of preliminary
competitions. Okay, girls, why don't
you tell us where you're coming from.

CONTESTANTS.
OH WHAT A NIGHT
OH WHAT A NIGHT
OH WHAT A NIGHT
OH WHAT A NIGHT

CONTESTANTS.
IT'S OUR BIRTHRIGHT AND DUTY
TO WORK HARD AT BEAUTY
AND WE'RE PROUD, PROUD, PROUD!

MISS DEEP SOUTH.
I'm proud to be a daughter
Of dear old Dixie Land
Where folks are so hospitable
They always lend a hand
You'll never hear a rude word
Coming from my mouth
I always strive for charm and grace
(SHE reveals her "MISS DEEP SOUTH" banner.)
For I am Miss Deep South.

MISS GREAT PLAINS.
I am proud of waving grain
Of fields ripe with corn

I'm Mother Nature's daughter
And greet her every morn
I cultivate the land
And nurse it like the rains
I sow the seed and reap the wheat
(Reveals her banner.)
For I am Miss Great Plains
MISS BIBLE BELT.
I'm proud to represent
The values of the Lord
For He spreads love all over
With His terrible swift sword
I know He'll reward me
'Cause in His house I've dwelt
I am proud to spread His word
(Reveals her banner.)
I'm Miss Bible Belt.
CONTESTANTS.
WE'RE THE PRIDE OF THIS GREAT COUNTRY
WE STAND OUT IN A CROWD
THOUGH WE'RE NOT ALL COLLEGIANS
WE'RE BEST IN OUR REGIONS
AND WE'RE PROUD, PROUD...
MISS TEXAS.
I am proud of plenty
Especially of my state
Where losers just skeedaddle
And winners congregate
Those who don't adore us
Truly do perplex us
I'm a button-bustin' lone-star gal
(Reveals her banner.)
And proud to be Miss Texas
MISS WEST COAST.
I am proud of living
On the San Andreas fault
I'd rather live life on the edge
Than safely in a vault

MISS WEST COAST. (cont.)
Of all the lives I've ever lived
I like this the most
I'm free, I'm me, it's meant to be
(Reveals her banner.)
For I am Miss West Coast
MISS INDUSTRIAL NORTHEAST.
I'm proud that Lady Liberty
Asked for the tired and poor
We're a land of many nations
And there's always room for more
When my relations came here
Their opportunities increased
I'm the pride of progress—
(Reveals her banner.)
Miss Industrial Northeast

(Dance Break.)

FRANKIE. *(Over end of dance break.)* There they are, ladies and gentlemen—our six semi-finalists! Each and every one a natural born female! Let's show the girls that we're pretty darn proud of them!!

FRANKIE.	**CONTESTANTS.**
THEY ARE NATURAL BORN FEMALES	WE ARE NATURAL BORN FEMALES
AND THE WANT TO SING IT LOUD	WE'RE NATURAL BORN FEMALES
THEY ARE NATURAL BORN FEMALES	WE'RE NATURAL BORN FEMALES
AND THEY'RE PROUD, PROUD, PROUD!	WE'RE NATURAL BORN FEMALES
	WE'RE AAH AAH AAH AAH NATURAL BORN FEMALES
	WE'RE NATURAL BORN FEMALES
	AND WE'RE PROUD, PROUD, PROUD
	WE HAVE ALL THE RIGHT

        CONTESTANTS. (cont.)
         EQUIPMENT
        BY NATURE WE'RE
         ENDOWED
        WE HAVE GOT EFFERVES-
         CENCE
        IT'S OUR GLAMOUR-
         ESSENCE
        AND WE'RE PROUD,
         PROUD, PROUD

(CONTESTANTS and FRANKIE salute and sing:)

  ALL.
AMERICA, YOU MADE US INTO
WHAT WE ARE TODAY
  FRANKIE.
THEY'RE NATURAL BORN FEMALES
  ALL.
MADE IN THE U.S.A.!!!!

(CONTESTANTS exit.)

(MUSIC #3 — "NATURAL BORN FEMALES" playoff)

FRANKIE. What girls! What an audience! What beauty! One of these lovely ladies is going to win the coveted and, I might add, lucrative contract to be next year's Miss Glamouresse! Of course she has to be gorgeous. But Miss Glamouresse must also be talented and have a charismatic personality that can withstand the probing scrutiny of the television cameras. And speaking of probing scrutiny, let's meet our judges!

(MUSIC #4 — JUDGES' INTRO)

(FRANKIE introduces five audience members from the first row as judges, using the following bios which he reads from index cards.)

FRANKIE. (cont.) Frances Tetley-Jones — head plumber at Windsor Castle and primary source for the best-selling, tell-all exposé,

Royal Flush! (Indicating audience member.) And they dare to say your book is a tissue of lies!

Poet Laureate of Hallmark Greeting Cards and author of "Love is a Special Kind of Specialness" — Emily Lloyd-Twee [Everett Lloyd-Twee if a man.] *(FRANKIE greets her.)* It's so nice to know you care enough. *(Going on to the next JUDGE.)*

Fresh from her appearance on "Oprah" where she told the tragic story of her 20-minute love affair with Elvis Presley — Cheryl Willa Klime! *(FRANKIE greets her.)* You're even lovelier in person. *(Moving to a WOMAN.)*

Her nation-wide crusades have made her a household word — the author of *Hello, God, You Don't Know Me But...* — Mary Beth Clawhammer! *(Greeting her.)* I'm halfway through your book and I think it's divine. *(Introducing the next JUDGE, preferably a bald man.)*

And last, but certainly not least, Herbert Fleck — hero to millions for leading the class-action suit against the manufacturers of "Rub-and-Grow Hair Fertilizer"! *(Winding up.)* Let's hear it, ladies and gentlemen, for our distinguished beauty panel!

(Applause and music tag.)

FRANKIE. (cont.) The contestants will compete in the following categories: evening gown, talent, swim-wear, physical fitness and beauty-crisis counseling. Plus — each girl will participate in our Spokesmodel Competition, to demonstrate her ability to speak effectively about the Glamouresse line. And now to kick off the Spokesmodel spots, here's Kitty-Bob Ames — Miss Texas!

(FRANKIE exits.)

(MUSIC #5 — SPOKESMODEL #1)

(MISS TEXAS appears in the "Spokesmodel Spot" wearing a frilly make-up smock, which the other CONTESTANTS will also wear.)

MISS TEXAS. Day in, day out, morning, noon and night, rush, rush, rush. C'est la vie for us modern women on the go, isn't it? And sometimes we don't even take the time for a snack, let alone a balanced meal. But, quelle surprise, once again it's Glamouresse to the rescue. They created LipSnack, color and calories in one attractive cylinder. *(Displaying a painter's palette featuring the different shades.)* Available in twenty-seven shades and flavors, from Roast Beef Red to Poached Salmon Pink. *(Opening an enormous lipstick.)* Now, simply apply as you would any common ordinary lipstick and then just taste the difference — Yum! And a single application of LipSnack contains twice the iron in a pound of calves liver. It's the prettiest protein you'll ever eat. Naturellement, from Glamouresse.

(MISS TEXAS exits as FRANKIE enters.)

FRANKIE. Thank you, Miss Texas, for setting such a high standard for the Spokesmodel Competition. Now let's see all our contestants compete in Evening Gowns — the perfect opportunity for me to tell them how I feel about them, not just as contestants, but as people.

(MUSIC #6 — "SOMETHING EXTRA")

(MISS DEEP SOUTH, MISS GREAT PLAINS and MISS WEST COAST enter one at a time in their evening gowns as FRANKIE sings the first verse.)

FRANKIE. (cont.)
YOU'VE GOT LOOKS
I MEAN A LOT
AND WHO COULD MEASURE ALL THE TALENT THAT
   YOU'VE GOT
YOU'VE GOT CHARM
AND YOU'VE GOT GRACE
AND ALL YOUR INNER BEAUTY SHOWS UP ON YOUR FACE
YOU'VE GOT EVERYTHING YOU NEED FROM A TO Z
YOU'VE GOT IT ALL
PLUS SOMETHING EXTRA

(During the next verse, MISS BIBLE BELT, MISS INDUSTRIAL NORTHEAST and MISS TEXAS enter one at a time.)

FRANKIE. (cont.)
A CERTAIN STYLE
A CERTAIN FLAIR
A CERTAIN GLOW THAT PUTS THE "OH" IN DEB-O-NAIR
YOU'VE GOT ALLURE
YOU'VE GOT FINESSE
THE GLAMOUR THAT'S THE ESSENCE OF MISS
     GLAMOURESSE
YOU'RE A MEMBER OF A SUPER-SPECIAL BREED
BORN TO SUCCEED
WITH SOMETHING EXTRA
YOU'RE BOUND TO BE A MOVER AND A SHAKER
BUT DON'T FORGET TO THANK YOUR LUCKY STARS
AND THANK YOUR MAKER
FOR THE THING YOU'VE GOT
THAT GIVES YOU SOMETHING MORE
YES, THANK THEM FOR
THAT SOMETHING EXTRA

(As the CONTESTANTS parade down the runway one-by-one modeling their gowns, FRANKIE reads biographical information from index cards.)

FRANKIE. (cont.) Miss Deep South, Laurinda Summerford, is a sophomore at Miss Frink's Female Academy where she is carrying a double-major in home economics and cancer research. Other interests include collecting clown memorabilia and organizing Right-to-Life rallies. Upon graduating, she would like to work to fight cancer where it begins. And that's in the home. *(MISS DEEP SOUTH crosses to FRANKIE after her parade down the runway.)* Laurinda, I understand you do some semi-professional acting.

MISS DEEP SOUTH. That's right. In my hometown of Valdosta, Georgia. I'm practically a fixture at the Drama Diner.

FRANKIE. Who'd suspect from looking at you that you do cancer research?

MISS DEEP SOUTH. I know. But I do. And it means even more to me than my acting.

FRANKIE. Why?

MISS DEEP SOUTH. Because acting can make people forget their pain for a little while, but cancer research can make them forget it permanently... eventually... maybe.

FRANKIE.

SHE'S SOMETHING EXTRA!

Miss Industrial Northeast, Consuela Manuela Rafaella Lopez, is a native American dish with a generous helping of spice from her Latin heritage. As the sole support of her family, she has not enjoyed the luxury of formal education. Consuela is currently studying hair-styling by mail while working as a receptionist at a woman's detention center. She has personally attended Macy's Thanksgiving Day parade. *(To MISS INDUSTRIAL NORTHEAST, who crosses to him.)* I see from my notes that you study hair-styling by mail. That must be difficult.

MISS INDUSTRIAL NORTHEAST. Oh, yes. It's hard to find heads for my homework. Thank goodness for the girls at the detention center.

FRANKIE. What exactly do you do there?

MISS INDUSTRIAL NORTHEAST. Oh, I'm just a temp but they'd like to have me on a permanent basis.

FRANKIE. Do the girls there know you're here tonight?

MISS INDUSTRIAL NORTHEAST. Oh yes. They made my earrings in the machine shop!

FRANKIE. They certainly did!

SHE'S SOMETHING EXTRA

A native of Oklahoma, Miss Bible Belt, Ruth Anne Ruth, is a scholarship student at Bob Jones University. Her majors are business administration and the Book of Lamentations. In the future she hopes to spread the gospel through telemarketing. Her hobbies include prayer and fasting. *(As MISS BIBLE BELT crosses to him.)* Miss Bible Belt, what is your beauty secret?

MISS BIBLE BELT. It's no secret. Consider the lilies of the field. If the Lord takes care of them why should I worry about oily skin?

FRANKIE. Do you feel any conflict between your religious convictions and your desire to be Miss Glamouresse?

MISS BIBLE BELT. No, I do not.

FRANKIE. You don't?

MISS BIBLE BELT. No, I do not.

FRANKIE. And who can argue with that!
SHE'S SOMETHING EXTRA

Born in a barn in Keokuk, Iowa, Bonnie Louise Cutlett, Miss Great Plains, is never so happy as when she's breeding livestock. Though she has never strayed far from hearth and home, Bonnie was Grand Prize Winner at the Iowa State Fair for her recipe for Iced Tea. She is compiling a cook-book called *Let's Get Creative with Marshmallow Fluff*. Her favorite color is beige. *(To MISS GREAT PLAINS.)* They tell me you've performed with the U.S.O.

MISS GREAT PLAINS. That's right — at the V.A. hospital is Des Moines. I've performed for servicemen, shut-ins and for people who are dying.

FRANKIE. They must be very glad to see you.

MISS GREAT PLAINS. Oh yes. Some of them haven't been entertained for eight to ten years.

FRANKIE. That's a long time without entertainment!

MISS GREAT PLAINS. Not in Des Moines.

FRANKIE.
SHE'S SOMETHING EXTRA

Miss West Coast, Karma Quinn, an est graduate, is a sales representative at the Spiritual Clearing House. Her hobbies include tie-dying fashions for Malibu Barbie, fire-walking and experiencing her many reincarnations. Karma is a double Gemini, and in the future she intends to live in the past. *(To MISS WEST COAST.)* I understand you've lived a lot of past lives.

MISS WEST COAST. Yes we have. At last count it was over a dozen.

FRANKIE. Boy, you must have some Christmas card list!

MISS WEST COAST. What?

FRANKIE. I know you're in there, Karma, I can hear you breathing.

MISS WEST COAST. Am I breathing too loud?

FRANKIE. *(Sighing.)* No, honey. *(Singing.)*
I LOVE YOU JUST THE WAY YOU ARE.

MISS WEST COAST. What?

FRANKIE.
SHE'S SOMETHING EXTRA

Miss Texas, Kitty-Bob Ames, began studying tap dancing at the age of three on her father's ranch with an instructor flown in weekly from New York. Despite her busy schedule as a party consultant, she still finds time to work with the beauty-impaired. She is the first girl to win the Texas Triple Crown of Beauty: Miss Spurs and Saddle, Miss Petroleum By-Products and Tally-Ho Princess of the El Paso Gun Club. *(To MISS TEXAS.)* So this is not your first beauty pageant — far from it!

MISS TEXAS. You're right as usual, Frankie. And I may be prejudiced, but I think the Miss Glamouresse Pageant has the most excitement, the most qualified judges and the best emcee in the business.

FRANKIE. It says here you work with the beauty impaired.

MISS TEXAS. Yes, I do. I really do. And you'd know why if you could see those unfortunate faces when I'm through with them.

FRANKIE. How generous of you.

MISS TEXAS. Well, it's like my Daddy always says, "We may have more money than God, but we don't have to act like it."

FRANKIE. Thank you Miss Texas and all our lovely girls! *(He sings as the CONTESTANTS "Ah" and parade past the judges.)*

YOU'RE BOUND TO BE A MOVER AND A SHAKER
BUT DON'T FORGET TO THANK YOUR LUCKY STARS
AND THANK YOUR MAKER
FOR THE THING YOU'VE GOT
THAT GIVES YOU SOMETHING MORE

YES, THANK THEM FOR
THAT SOMETHING EXTRA
Ladies and Gentlemen, The Evening Gown Competition!

(The curtain closes on the CONTESTANTS as they pose in high-fashion stances.)

FRANKIE. (cont.) If anyone has to have something extra it's Miss Glamouresse and here to show us how she measures up in the Spokesmodel category is Bonnie Louise Cutlett, Miss Great Plains.

(FRANKIE exits.)

(MUSIC #7 — SPOKESMODEL #2)

MISS GREAT PLAINS. *(Entering into Spokesmodel Spot.)* You're a woman. You're aware of your appearance and the importance of keeping every hair in place. But you're not just a hair-do and a heartbeat. You have a conscience too. So you're also aware of the environment and the importance of maintaining a beautiful natural backdrop for your loveliness. That's why Glamouresse is introducing Hair Aware with Air Repair — the styling spray for the woman with a head on her shoulders. Now we can repair the damage we all do to the ozone layer every time we whip our locks into shape. After spraying the finishing coat on your do-of-the-day, *(Spraying a more-than-healthy amount on her "do".)* flip over the virtually asbestos-free canister to the Air Repair end, point and shoot. *(Protecting herself with a frilly welding mask.)* That ole ozone layer will be fit as a fiddle in no time at all. Oh, don't forget to keep Air Repair out of the reach of children and pets. And, please, look away from the spray. "If it ain't broke, don't fix it" — but if it *is* — use Hair Aware with Air Repair from Glamouresse.

(MISS GREAT PLAINS exits as FRANKIE enters.)

FRANKIE. You know, folks, a wise man once said, "Beauty is as beauty does." So let's see what these girls can do in our talent cavalcade. If there's one girl that can start us off with a bang, it's Miss Texas, Kitty-Bob Ames, so let's see just how much Kitty-Bob "Ames" to please.

(MUSIC #8 — MISS TEXAS TALENT)

MISS TEXAS. *(Is revealed wearing a cowgirl outfit, complete with pistols and is seated on a rolling hobby horse. Singing to the tune of "Home on the Range.")*

MY STATE IS THE BEST
BUT WE NEVER CAN REST
'TIL THE VARMINTS ARE ALL ON THE RUN

WE ROPE AND WE SHOOT
EVERY CRITTER AND BRUTE
'CAUSE THAT'S HOW THE OLD WEST WAS WON

(SHE explodes into a frantic tap-dance, starting on her hobby horse.)

CHICKEN IN THE BREAD-PAN
PICKIN' OUT DOUGH

(The routine incorporates rope twirling, clogging and climaxes with a sharp-shooter routine. SHE bows as the talent curtain closes in front of her and FRANKIE enters.)

FRANKIE. Thank you, Miss Texas, for being such a pro! And now Miss Great Plains, Bonnie Louise Cutlett, will present a dramatic recitation of her own composition.

(FRANKIE exits.)

(MUSIC #9 — MISS GREAT PLAINS TALENT)

MISS GREAT PLAINS. *(Enters and delivers the following with great passion, wearing a glamorized farmer outfit.)*
I am a handful of dirt
A field of waving grain
A thousand acres of virgin forest
A raging river
A babbling brook
I am the land.

I am the land — Shhhh! Listen.

(When the audience doesn't appear to be listening hard enough.)

When you pierce me with your tools—
Do you hear me crying?
When you gnaw at me with your big machines—
Do you hear my screams?

MISS GREAT PLAINS. (cont.)
When you reap my bounty, year after year after year—
Do you hear the howling wind
Bearing me away into the angry sky?

(Again, SHE is disappointed in the response.)

Well, do you?

You sing "America the Beautiful," oh, yes!
Even as you make me America the Ugly!
You *say* you love me
Even as you ravage me!
I trusted you
But you have used me and forsaken me
So that now I am racked with pain
Waste, disease, desolation, pollution
And rot.

You must choose.

Yes you!
What's it to be, America—
Pollution or paradise?

(As "Battle Hymn of the Republic" is played by the orchestra.)

Yes. Oh, yes.
Come, let us love one another again
Before it is too late
We belong together, you and I
For you are the good people of the United States of America
And I?
I am the land!

(MISS GREAT PLAINS bows, then exits as FRANKIE enters.)

FRANKIE. Now here's Ruth Anne Ruth, Miss Bible Belt, in her Spokesmodel Spot with Glamouresse's solution to a vexing problem.

(FRANKIE exits as MISS BIBLE BELT enters.)

(MUSIC #10 — SPOKESMODEL #3)

MISS BIBLE BELT. Do you have an enlarged pore, cleft, pit or indentation in your skin? Ordinary make-up won't cover that up. That's why Glamouresse invented Smooth-as-Marble Facial Spackle. *(She displays a frilly cold-cream size jar.)* That's right—facial spackle, the revolutionary new make-up for a deep-down cover-up. Of course, the action of Smooth-as-Marble's micro-emulsion cannot be seen with the naked eye, but Smooth-as-Marble fills in the pores of your skin just like this spackle... *(SHE reveals a delicate trowel with spackle.)* fills in the pits in this wallboard. *(SHE pulls out a banged-up piece of wallboard and smooths a gob of spackle over an area of it.)* Naturally, Smooth-as-Marble comes complete with its own carrying case and applicator, in your choice of *faux* gold, *faux* silver, or *faux* stainless steel. Also available in Heavy Duty for gouges and scars. *(SHE pulls out a bucket-size version.)* So if you have unpretty cracks in your plaster — just pull into our surface station and say "Fill 'em up!" — with Glamouresse.

(MISS BIBLE BELT exits as FRANKIE enters.)

FRANKIE. Thank you, Miss Bible Belt.. *(Setting a small stool in place for MISS DEEP SOUTH.)* Our next entrant in the Talent Portion of our Competition, Laurinda Summerford, Miss Deep South, will present a salute to Dixie with a little help from her friends.

(FRANKIE exits.)

(MUSIC #11 — MISS DEEP SOUTH TALENT)

(Entering to the strains of "Beautiful Dreamer," MISS DEEP SOUTH features a Scarlett O'Hara gown which hides her puppets.)

MISS DEEP SOUTH.
BEAUTIFUL DREAMER
WAKE UNTO ME
STARLIGHT AND DEWDROPS ARE WAITING FOR THEE
   Land! I'm so tired of doing, doing, doing. How I long for that
gracious time before the War Between the States, a time when a lady
didn't have to do all her doin' herself. A time of cavaliers and cotton
fields—

*(Now attempting ventriloquism in an "old lady" voice, SHE brings
   up, on one hand, an old, gray-haired Southern Belle puppet, OLD
   MISS JEANIE.)*

   (OLD MISS JEANIE.) — And me!
   MISS DEEP SOUTH. Why, Great Great Grandma Jeanie,
where'd you come from?
   (OLD MISS JEANIE.)
I COME FROM ALABAMA
JUST TO SIT HERE ON YOUR KNEE
I COME TO TELL YOU ALL ABOUT
THE WAY THINGS USED TO BE

OH, LAURINDA!
OH, DON'T YOU CRY FOR ME
I COME FROM ALABAMA...

*(Now "ventriloquizing" in an "old man" voice, SHE brings up, on
   the other hand, an old, gray-haired "Colonel Sanders" puppet—
   COLONEL.)*

   (COLONEL.)
AND DON'T FORGET ABOUT ME!
   MISS DEEP SOUTH. Why, Great Great Grandaddy Colonel
Summerford! What are you doing here?
   (COLONEL.) I came here 'cause I been a-dreamin'!

(COLONEL hiccups.)

(**OLD MISS JEANIE.**) And a-drinkin' too!

(OLD MISS JEANIE "boo-hoos.")

MISS DEEP SOUTH. *(Whispering to COLONEL.)* Sing that song.

(**COLONEL.**) *(Trying to get on OLD MISS JEANIE's good side.)*
I DREAM OF JEANIE
WITH THE LIGHT BROWN HAIR
BORNE LIKE A VAPOR
ON THE SOFT SUMMER AIR

(**OLD MISS JEANIE.**) Why, Colonel, how sweet!

(**COLONEL.**) Well, of course, that was before you lost your looks.

MISS DEEP SOUTH. *(Scolding.)* Now, Colonel, Grandma Jeanie was a great beauty in her time.

(**COLONEL.**) In her time maybe, but it's your time now, Laurinda.

(**OLD MISS JEANIE.**) For once in his life he's right. You're the pretty one now, Laurinda honey.

MISS DEEP SOUTH. Oh, you two! Stop it!!!

(**COLONEL.**) It's her lily-white skin that's so lovely.

(**OLD MISS JEANIE.**) No, you old coot! It's her sparklin' Dixie eyes!

MISS DEEP SOUTH. Oh fiddle-dee-dee. You're gonna make me blush, I swear. Let's stop this foolishness and let's go to the races!

(**COLONEL.**) And what races might they be, Laurinda?

(**OLD MISS JEANIE.**) You old fool! You know perfectly well!
CAMPTOWN LADIES SING DIS SONG
DOO-DAH
DOO-DAH!

MISS DEEP SOUTH.
CAMPTOWN RACETRACK FIVE MILES LONG

(**COLONEL.**)
OH DE DOO-DAH DAY

(**OLD MISS JEANIE.**)
I COME DOWN DAH WID MY HAT CAVED IN

MISS DEEP SOUTH.
DOO-DAH
DOO-DAH

(COLONEL.)
COME BACK HOME WID A BELLY FULL O' GIN
  (OLD JEANIE.)
OH DE DOO-DAH DAY
  (COLONEL.)
GWINE TO
  (OLD JEANIE.)
RUN ALL
  MISS DEEP SOUTH.
NIGHT
GWINE TO
  (OLD JEANIE.)
RUN ALL
  (COLONEL.)
DAY
  (OLD JEANIE.)
I'LL BET MY MONEY ON DE BOBTAIL NAG
  (COLONEL.)
SOMEBODY BET ON
  (OLD JEANIE.)
SOMEBODY BET ON
  MISS DEEP SOUTH.
SOMEBODY BET ON DE BAY — HEY!

(After bowing, SHE turns Upstage revealing that her antebellum gown has no back. But SHE is wearing frilly pantaloons. Feigning embarrassment, SHE runs Offstage as FRANKIE enters.)

FRANKIE. Our next contestant created her talent from the ground up and as you'll see the sky's the limit. Here is Karma Quinn, Miss West Coast, in an interpretive dance entitled, "The Seven Ages of Me!"

(FRANKIE exits.)

(MUSIC #12 —MISS WEST COAST TALENT — TAPE.)

(MISS WEST COAST is revealed Upstage. SHE performs a dance moderne which shows a history of her evolution, beginning in a Martha-Graham-style body bag. Her dance is divided into the following sections — each of which SHE announces. **NOTE:** *The accompanying tape includes a rehearsal track indicating where the spoken lines occur in the music.)*

MISS WEST COAST. *(Crawling out of her body bag.)*
I am born.
I discover the world.
The world discovers me.
I fall in love.
I get hurt.
(SHE falls down.)
I search.

(A large hibachi grill is revealed Upstage. SHE "lights" the coals, then walks across them)

MISS WEST COAST. (cont.)
I die.
I am re-born.

(SHE goes through the cycle again, only much faster this time. Finally, SHE brings her cycle to an end with:)

MISS WEST COAST. (cont.)
Etcetera, etcetera, etcetera.

(The orchestra climaxes with a big "TA-DA!" and playoff. MISS WEST COAST exits as FRANKIE enters.)

FRANKIE. And now here's Karma Quinn, Miss West Coast, in her Spokesmodel Spot.

(FRANKIE exits.)

(MUSIC #13 — SPOKESMODEL #4)

MISS WEST COAST. *(Running back on wearing the Spokesmodel smock. SHE's out of breath from her dance, but gamely struggles through.)* Really. I'm a woman. I need to be fresh and feminine all day long. And now, for active women like me, deodorant protection is a snap! Glamouresse is proud to present "Snappin' Fresh," the very latest in feminine deodorant apparel. That's right, you *wear* it! There are three chic fashion accessories to choose from: headband, wrist strap, and pretty cameo choker. *(Each is a strip of fabric, elasticized, with Velcro on the ends and a plastic disc in the middle. SHE puts on all three.)* Now, whichever you choose, there's enough ionized inorganic material in each disc to deodorize the average active female for thirty-seven hours. Or we'll be very much surprised. And here's the fun part. To release the patented active ingredient, Sani-scent, all you have to do is snap! *(SHE grasps the plastic disc, pulls on the elasticized fabric, and snaps, in turn, the wrist strap, the choker, and the headband. Each snap is accompanied by a bizarre sound from the orchestra. The fragrance leaves her a bit dazed.)* 'Cause being fresh is a snap with "Snappin' Fresh" from Glamouresse.

(MISS WEST COAST exits as FRANKIE enters.)

FRANKIE. Contestants in the Miss Glamouresse Pageant are famous for the diversity of their talents. Here's Consuela Manuela Rafaella Lopez, Miss Industrial Northeast, with a Classical Fantasia in C Major!

(MUSIC #14 — MISS INDUSTRIAL NORTHEAST TALENT)

(MISS INDUSTRIAL NORTHEAST comes sailing out on roller skates with an accordion. SHE nearly rolls off the other side of the stage, but catches herself on the proscenium and pushes herself back Center. FRANKIE helps steady her and then exits. The BAND starts a polka vamp. MISS INDUSTRIAL NORTHEAST faces front, takes a deep breath and begins to play. Her contribution to the "Classical Fantasia" is an endlessly repeated C Major scale — sometimes fast, sometimes slow, but always played with great concentra-

*tion and effort. Against this, the BAND weaves a medley of well-
known classical themes. Halfway through, the tempo changes to
a furious "Sabre Dance" feel, and MISS INDUSTRIAL NORTH-
EAST begins to skate around the stage playing, not her beloved
scale, but the "Skaters' Waltz!" This virtuoso feat is climaxed with
a final airing of the C major scale, and the routine ends in triumph.
Curtain closes in front of her as FRANKIE enters.)*

FRANKIE. As our final contestant in the Talent Competition,
Miss Bible Belt, Ruth Anne Ruth, will give us a new taste of that old
time religion.

*(FRANKIE exits as MISS BIBLE BELT enters and takes FRANKIE's
wireless microphone.)*

*(MUSIC #15 — MISS BIBLE BELT TALENT — "BANKING ON
JESUS")*

MISS BIBLE BELT.
NOW, I DON'T NEED NO WALL STREET JOURNAL
I'M BANKING ON JESUS
MY WEALTH EARNS INT'REST THAT'S ETERNAL
I'M BANKING ON JESUS
HE CAN PASS ALL ETHICS TESTS
AND SAFE WITH HIM MY NEST EGG RESTS
THE LORD SAVES, THEN RE-INVESTS
I'M BANKING ON JESUS

BANKING ON JESUS
OH, WHAT A FRIEND
THE BIBLE'S MY BANKBOOK
HUMBLY I SPEND
NOW THERE IS NOTHING
I CAN'T AFFORD
MY CO-SIGNER'S
JESUS THE LORD

MY INVESTMENTS ARE PROTECTED

I'M BANKING ON JESUS
MY HOLDINGS HAVE BEEN RESURRECTED
I'M BANKING ON JESUS
AND WHEN I FACE THAT BURNING SHRUB
WHILE OTHERS MEET BEELZEBUB
I'LL CASH IN MY CHRISTMAS CLUB
I'M BANKING ON JESUS

BANKING ON JESUS
OH, WHAT A FRIEND
THE BIBLE'S MY BANKBOOK
HUMBLY I SPEND
MY CREDIT RATING SUDDENLY SOARED
MY CO-SIGNER'S
JESUS THE LORD

Brothers and Sisters, I was not always the shining symbol of success you see standing before you. There was a time when I'd reached rock bottom — my mortgage was overdue, my car was about to be repossessed, *(Starting to cry.)* I didn't even have the money to buy mascara! But I asked the Lord for help and He looked at my bottom line. He expanded my portfolio. He routed the devil in a hostile takeover! The Good Book says, "Ask and ye shall receive." And may I add:

Once you receive it
You'll need fiscal advice
With the Lord as your broker
You can buy Paradise!

(The curtain opens to reveal a set of melody bells on a table. MISS BIBLE BELT gives a ringing affirmation of faith. Then SHE winds it up in a gospel frenzy, getting the audience to clap along.)

MISS BIBLE BELT. (cont.)
BANKING ON JESUS
OH, WHAT A FRIEND
THE BIBLE'S MY BANKBOOK
HUMBLY I SPEND

MY CREDIT RATING
SUDDENLY SOARED
MY CO-SIGNER
I said MY
I said MY CO-SIGN—
I said MY CO-SIGNER IS
I said MY CO-SIGNER IS JESUS
I said MY CO-SIGNER IS JESUS THE

(MISS BIBLE BELT breaks into rapid-fire babble—"speaking in tongues"—something like:)

A shanda-ma-lay coshonki desdelah mishkalanto hey!

(Looking to the heavens from whence that came with a sort of how-do-you-do-that? look, then bringing it home.)

LORD!

(MISS BIBLE BELT bows, then exits as FRANKIE enters.)

FRANKIE. Thank you, Miss Bible Belt. Somewhere in heaven there's an angel without a voice.

(MUSIC #16 — SPOKESMODEL #5)

FRANKIE. (cont.) You know, every girl needs something extra from Glamouresse. And here's Miss Deep South, Laurinda Summerford, with their latest beauty breakthrough.

(FRANKIE exits as MISS DEEP SOUTH enters.)

MISS DEEP SOUTH. How often has this happened to you? You have a date with Him, that special someone. You take out your compact for a last-minute touch-up. And then it happens. You powder your nose and the front of your dress too! You try to brush it off and it just gets worse! And then, of course... *(A doorbell rings.)* Your whole evening is ruined! Well thanks to Glamouresse, this tragedy can be avoided. Now there's Puff 'n' Vac—pressed powder, powder puff, and powerful vacuum in one glamorous compact. Watch as I dramatize. *(SHE pulls out a black bib and puts it around her neck.)* Just apply your powder as usual. *(SHE powders her chin and spills a lot of powder on the bib.)* Ooops! Next, pass the built-in nozzle over your face, dress, legs, *(She vacuums the powder off the bib.)* —any place stray powder may hide. Puff 'n' Vac does the dirty work, and all that's left is a more beautiful you. No wonder more and more glamorous women are Glamouresse women.

(MISS DEEP SOUTH exits.)

(MUSIC #17 — "IT'S GOTTA BE VENUS")

   FRANKIE. *(Offstage.)* Do you worry about the new millennium? Do you fret about your beauty future? Do you wonder how Glamouresse will meet the challenge of looking good in Outer Space? Well we're way ahead of you! Introducing—Glamouresse's new cutting-edge beauty agenda—Project Venus 3000! *(He enters in a space suit to sci-fi underscoring and sings.)*

MERCURY, JUPITER, SATURN OR MARS
WHERE HAVE I LANDED OUT HERE IN THE STARS
U*RAN*US
OR *U*RANUS, NEPTUNE OR PLUTO
SUDDENLY I KNOW WHERE I'VE BEEN *EN ROUTE,* OH—

I'M IN A PLACE THAT'S VERY RARE
I FEEL A THRILL BEYOND COMPARE
I KNOW THAT NOTHING ANYWHERE
COULD EVER COME BETWEEN US
IT'S GOTTA BE LO-OVE
IT'S GOTTA BE VENUS!

AND THERE'S NO FRICTION IN THE AIR
AN ATMOSPHERE WE'RE MEANT TO SHARE
OLD FRIENDS WE MEET THEY STOP AND STARE
AS IF THEY'D NEVER SEEN US

IT'S GOTTA BE LO-OVE
IT'S GOTTA BE VENUS!

I'VE NEVER SEEN YOU LOOK
SO OUT OF THIS WORLD
JUST LIKE AN OPEN BOOK
OR A FLAG THAT'S UNFURLED
I'M SPINNING ON MY AXIS
LIKE A PLANET THAT'S BEEN TWIRLED
IT'S GOTTA BE LOVE
IT'S GOTTA BE LOVE
IT'S GOTTA BE VENUS

MY HEART IS ROCKETING IN RINGS
I BOUNCE AS THOUGH MY FEET HAD SPRINGS
AND WHEN THEY SAY THAT LOVE HAS WINGS
CERTAINLY THEY MEAN US
IT'S GOTTA BE LO-OVE
IT'S GOTTA BE...
(Calling to the ship.)
   Girls, what in the universe is taking you so long?

(Curtain opens to reveal exterior of a space ship with six portholes.)

   FRANKIE. (cont.) You're going to be late for your own Future!

(FRANKIE exits as the CONTESTANTS' faces appear in the portholes of the space ship as they raise mini-blinds covering the portholes. The CONTESTANTS wear towels wrapped around their hair.)

   CONTESTANTS.
WHAT DO I WEAR TO A BRAND NEW PLANET?
SHOULD I BRING FLATS OR HIGH HEELS?
SHOULD I BE SOFT
OR AS HARD AS GRANITE
WHO KNOWS HOW AN ALIEN FEELS?

MISS DEEP SOUTH.
SHOULD MY SHOULDERS LOOK LARGE
   MISS INDUSTRIAL NORTHEAST.
OR SHOULD THEY LOOK SKINNY?
   MISS TEXAS.
HOW SHOULD I FIX MY HAIR?
   MISS BIBLE BELT.
SHOULD I CHOOSE MAXI?
   MISS GREAT PLAINS.
OR MIDI?
   MISS WEST COAST.
OR MINI?
   CONTESTANTS.
WILL A SCALY ALIEN EVEN CARE?
   GREAT PLAINS, TEXAS, DEEP SOUTH.
WILL WE NEED SUN SCREEN?
   WEST COAST, NORTHEAST, BIBLE BELT.
OR WILL WE NEED MOON BLOCK?
   FRANKIE. *(Entering.)*
GIRLS! LOOK AT THE MOON CLOCK!
YOU'VE ONLY GOT A MINUTE TO GET GORGEOUS AND
   GET OUT!
   CONTESTANTS.
THAT'S TIME ENOUGH TO SHOW
WHAT GLAMOURESSE IS ALL ABOUT!

(THEY lower the mini-blinds.)

   FRANKIE.
PROJECT VENUS 3000
IS ALL GLAMOURESSE'S
AND IT'S GONE TO THEIR HEADS
JUST LOOK AT THEIR TRESSES!

*(The CONTESTANTS emerge from the spaceship having doffed their
   towels. But their hair is now Glamouresse pink and set exactly as
   their previous wigs. THEY are wearing "space" make-up smocks.)*

FRANKIE.
I'VE NEVER SEEN YOU LOOK
SO OUT OF THIS WORLD

JUST LIKE AN OPEN BOOK
OR A FLAG THAT'S
   UNFURLED
I'M SPINNING ON MY AXIS
LIKE A PLANET THAT'S BEEN
   TWIRLED
IT'S GOTTA BE LOVE
   CONTESTANTS.
IT'S GOTTA BE LOVE

CONTESTANTS.
SEEN YOU LOOK
IT'S A BIG, WIDE
   WONDERFUL WORLD
LIKE AN OPE— OPEN BOOK
VENUS WOW!

WHEEEE

   FRANKIE.
IT'S GOTTA BE VENUS
IT'S GOTTA BE VENUS
MY HEAR IS ROCKETING IN
   RINGS
I BOUNCE AS THOUGH MY
   FEET HAD SPRINGS
AND WHEN THEY SAY THAT
   LOVE HAS WINGS
CERTAINLY THEY MEAN US
IT'S GOTTA BE LO-OVE
IT'S GOTTA BE VENUS
IT'S GOTTA BE LOVE
IT'S GOTTA BE LOVE
   ALL.
IT'S LOVE, LOVE, LOVE, LOVE
LOVE, LOVE, LOVE, LOVE, LOVE
   CONTESTANTS.
IT'S GOTTA BE!

CONTESTANTS.
GOTTA BE VENUS

AHHHHH

BOING! BOING! BOING!

IT'S FLYING AWAY

LOVE!
VENUS
IT'S GOTTA BE LOVE
IT'S GOTTA BE LOVE

   FRANKIE.
VENUS

VENUS

CONTESTANTS.
GOT TO BE
GOT TO BE VENUS
GOT TO BE
GOT TO BE VENUS

FRANKIE. (cont.)	**CONTESTANTS.** (cont.)
VENUS	GOT TO BE
	GOT TO BE VENUS
	GOT TO BE
	GOT TO BE VENUS
	GOT TO BE
	GOT TO BE VENUS
	GOT TO BE
	GOT TO BE VENUS

ALL.
LOVE, LOVE
VENUS!

(On the button of the number, the CONTESTANTS remove their space
smocks and reveal their swim-suits and banners. Then THEY exit
into space ship.)

FRANKIE. People of Venus, we'd like to give you a closer look
at our contestants. And now, as they display their wares in the swim-
suit competition, we'll hear from their minds as well.

(MUSIC #18 — SWIMSUIT COMPETITION)

(FRANKIE exits as the CONTESTANTS parade down the runway
one at a time in swim-suits, now wearing their regular wigs. We
hear their voices on tape as if we're listening to their thoughts.
After each such moment, the CONTESTANT returns to the space
ship, raises the mini-blinds and peeks out of a porthole.)

MISS DEEP SOUTH. *(On Tape.)* I believe in traditional gentility,
modulated tones and graciousness of manner. If the governments of
the universe would lay down their guns and pick up the correct fork,
the solar system would be a more beautiful place in which to live.
   MISS GREAT PLAINS. *(On Tape.)* I believe in my Mom. Ever
since we entered the Lake Okabogi County Mother/Daughter Pageant, we've had a very special relationship, even though we didn't
win. Or even place. If I win tonight, I'm dedicating my tiara to just

one person — my best friend, my teacher — my Mom.

MISS WEST COAST. *(On Tape.)* I believe that everything is everything. I used to think that all men are brothers, but now I know that all people are persons. So all women are brothers too, and all men are sisters, and once in a while just about everybody is an uncle or a cousin. Like that.

MISS TEXAS. *(On Tape.)* I believe that a person is never so beautiful as when she stoops to help someone less fortunate. After all, true beauty doesn't reside in a pleasing face, a statuesque figure, or a shapely leg. True beauty resides in a helping hand and a generous heart.

MISS BIBLE BELT. *(On Tape.)* I believe in the beauty of abundance. The Lord has created so many cosmetics, it's downright sinful not to use them. If God gave you manna in the wilderness would you say, "I'm on a diet"? More is better.

MISS INDUSTRIAL NORTHEAST. *(On Tape.)* I believe that beauty is a rainbow. Does purple hate red? Does yellow tell orange not to move in next door? Does blue bash green and call it ugly names? Of course not! Let's take a lesson from the rainbow and allow all our colors to live side by side in harmony — like people.

FRANKIE. *(On Tape, Entering as the CONTESTANTS have.)* And I believe these girls deserve a great big hand! *(Now live on his microphone.)* Thank you, Ambassadors of Beauty. People of Venus, we envy you because living in a weightless environment, you never have to be concerned about being too heavy. But on Earth, we have to work at staying fit and trim—especially the gals. Now as they compete in the category of physical fitness, let's see how the girls of Earth go about their Beauty Work!

(FRANKIE exits as CONTESTANTS enter from space ship.)

(MUSIC #19 — "GIRL POWER")

CONTESTANTS. Five, Six, Seven, Eight! *(Aerobicising on individual step units.)*
WE'VE GOT THE POWER AND THE POWER IS FEMININE
GIRL POWER!
AND WITH THE POWER WE CAN CATCH SOMEONE MASCULINE
GIRL POWER!

IF YOU WANT A HUSBAND, IF YOU WANT A FLAME
FEEL THE BURN UNTIL YOU KNOW YOU CAN WIN
YEAH WORK IT OUT! AND TUCK YOUR TUMMY IN
IF YOU WANT A GUY
YOU'VE GOT THE POWER TO STAY THIN
GIRL POWER!
GIRL POWER!

(Dance break after which FRANKIE delivers towels and the CON-
TESTANTS daintily mop up.)

CONTESTANTS. (cont.)
NO MATTER WHAT COMPLAINTS YOU GET FROM GUYS
YOU KNOW THAT REALLY THEY ADORE IT
THEY KNOW THAT THEY'RE THE REASON FOR IT
JUST KEEP YOUR EYES UPON THE PRIZE!
(THEY go back into a final, frantic group work-out.)
WE'VE FOUND THE POWER AND IT'S BOTTOMLESS
'CAUSE AT GLAMOURESSE
WE TAKE THE POWER ALL THE WAY
GIRL POWER!
GIRL POWER!
WHEEE!   WHEEE!
WHEEE!   WHEEE!
GIRL POWER!

(Curtain on Outer Space.)

FRANKIE. *(Enters, now wearing tails.)* Gee, it's great to be back
on Earth. You know, it's a lot of fun to get all dressed up, but boy, it
sure feels good to be back in my street clothes.

(MUSIC #20 — SPOKESMODEL #6)

FRANKIE. (cont.) And now, to complete the Spokesmodel seg-
ment of the competition here's Consuela Manuela Rafaella Lopez,
Miss Industrial Northeast, with a beauty breakthrough that's newer
than tomorrow.

(FRANKIE exits as MISS INDUSTRIAL NORTHEAST enters.)

MISS INDUSTRIAL NORTHEAST. *(Wearing a kerchief around her hair.)* Freedom. Pretty important, isn't it? My hair is important to me — but so is freedom. That's why, on my all-American head, I use the energy-efficient, hair-curling system: Solar Rollers. *(SHE takes off the kerchief.)* The secret is in the panels. Solar panels. Funny-looking? Maybe. But instead of being chained to an old-fashioned curling iron, now I can jog, garden, paint the house, or just walk down the street and drop a postcard in the mailbox. *That's* freedom. Sometimes I even pick up Cinemax at no extra cost! And I can cook a frozen egg roll for a t.v. snack! *(SHE pulls a small egg roll out of one of the rollers.)* Mmmm. Now that's convenience! It's so natural: no kilowatts if you please! Just Mr. Sun, me and my Solar Rollers. Freedom? I spell it G-L-A-M-O *(SHE pauses for a second, not exactly sure, then looks over the counter where the name is printed.)* U-R-E-S-S-E. Freedom.

(MISS INDUSTRIAL NORTHEAST exits as FRANKIE enters.)

FRANKIE. Thank you, Miss Industrial Northeast! Ladies and gentlemen, we are so very proud to have a special guest backstage tonight, and that's Elizabeth Glamgauer-Meade, the founder of the house of Glamouresse. Though she no longer appears in public, Mrs. Glamgauer-Meade still reserves the right to select the finalists for the Miss Glamouresse Pageant and she is engaged in that difficult task right now. Boy oh boy, I wouldn't want to be in her heels. But while she's making her decisions, the girls have made a decision of their own. Momentarily, it will be my honor to make a special presentation — the Glamouresse Girlfriend Award. This prize is given to the most congenial contestant, the one girl the others would most like to have for a girlfriend, if only they had the time. Now, let's take one last look at all our deserving contestants.

(MUSIC #21 — GLAMOURESSE GIRLFRIEND)

(CONTESTANTS are revealed in their tea dresses, without their banners.)

FRANKIE. (cont.) This is the last time they'll all be together, maybe that's why they look lovelier than ever. And now, the winner of this year's Glamouresse Girlfriend Award, chosen by the girls themselves, is... [PLEASE **NOTE:** Depending on which ACTOR is better equipped to reappear as a new character (the REIGNING MISS GLAMOURESSE), the "Girlfriend Award" goes to either MISS INDUSTRIAL NORTHEAST or MISS WEST COAST] Miss West Coast, Karma Quinn! [**OR:** Miss Industrial Northeast, Consuela Manuela Rafaella Lopez!]

(The GIRLFRIEND AWARD WINNER stumbles forward as the CONTESTANTS applaud and scream. Genuinely moved and dumbfounded, SHE receives the award — a large frilly heart pillow which FRANKIE hangs around her neck — and stumbles back to her place.)

FRANKIE. (cont.) She's really touched — and Karma [Consuela], so are we. *(Looking offstage.)* I understand that Mrs. Glamgauer-Meade has reached her decision. May I have the envelope, please?

(MUSIC #22 — FINALISTS)

(Orchestra conductor cues timpani roll. A white-gloved hand delivers the envelope from Off-stage. FRANKIE opens it.)

FRANKIE. (cont.) And now, I don't want to keep you or the girls in suspense any longer. The finalists for Miss Glamouresse [UPCOMING YEAR] in reverse alphabetical order according to their regions are:

(As each FINALIST is announced, SHE steps Downstage to one side, leaving the Center clear. This announcement should happen so fast that no one has time to think.)

*[**NOTE:** If GIRLFRIEND AWARD WINNER is MISS INDUSTRIAL NORTHEAST, FRANKIE reads the following:)*

FRANKIE. (cont.)

Karma Quinn — Miss West Coast!

Kitty Bob Ames — Miss Texas!

Bonnie Louise Cutlett — Miss Great Plains!

Laurinda Summerford — Miss Deep South!

And our last finalist is... Ruth Anne Ruth — Miss Bible Belt!
Let's hear it for our five finalists!

*[NOTE: If GIRLFRIEND AWARD WINNER is MISS WEST COAST,
FRANKIE reads the following:]*

FRANKIE. (cont.)

Kitty Bob Ames — Miss Texas!

Consuela Manuela Rafaella Lopez — Miss Industrial Northeast!

Bonnie Louise Cutlett — Miss Great Plains!

Laurinda Summerford — Miss Deep South!

And our last finalist is... Ruth Anne Ruth — Miss Bible Belt!
Let's hear it for our five finalists!

*(Fanfare as curtain closes in front of GIRLFRIEND AWARD WIN-
NER standing forlornly with the heart pillow hanging around her
neck. FRANKIE moves the Glamouresse counter Center.)*

FRANKIE. (cont.) Congratulations, ladies, you've come a long
way and there's only a little bit further to go. Ladies, as you know,
one of Glamouresse's proudest philanthropic efforts is its twenty-
four hour toll-free Beauty Crisis Hotline. Women all over the country know they can dial 1-800-4-BEAUTY...

(MUSIC #23 — BEAUTY CRISIS HOTLINE)

FRANKIE. (cont.) *(He pulls out a phone with the Beauty Crisis
number 1-800-4-BEAUTY displayed on its base.)* ... for emergency
beauty counseling. Girls, for your final test this evening, we are ask-
ing you to respond to an actual Beauty Crisis Hotline call. When the
music stops and the phone rings, you're on the hot line! Ladies, if
you please.

*(A game of "musical phones" ensues. The CONTESTANTS circle
the phone, becoming increasingly competitive as their numbers
dwindle. When the music stops, the phone rings and each CON-
TESTANT picks it up as indicated, responding to the Five Women
Callers. The Callers' Voices are pre-recorded. As the CONTES-
TANTS start circling, FRANKIE says:)*

FRANKIE. (cont.) Round and round the Glamouresse phone
When it rings you're on your own!

(FRANKIE exits. Phone rings and MISS TEXAS answers.)

MISS TEXAS. Beauty Crisis Hotline. How may I help you?
FEMALE CALLER #1. (On Tape.) I am going to have the birth
of my baby recorded on video tape. What make-up should I wear for
this event?
MISS TEXAS. Well, you wouldn't want to wear anything shiny
or with glitter in it that might reflect in the cameras. May I suggest
something organic like Glamouresse's Natural Woman line. And if
that baby's a girl, it's never too soon to introduce her to Pretty Baby,
our special line for women under the age of five.

*(Same "musical phone" sequence, this time MISS GREAT PLAINS
confidently picks up the receiver.)*

MISS GREAT PLAINS. Hi! Thanks so much for calling!
FEMALE CALLER #2. (On Tape.) I live on a fixed income. I
love everything that Glamouresse makes, but I can't afford make-up
and medication for a life-threatening congenital condition. What
should I do?
MISS GREAT PLAINS. What should you do? I honestly don't
know. Maybe if you took a teeney bit less medication, you could
afford a teeney bit more makeup. And at least you wouldn't look so
sick. Good luck.

*(MISS GREAT PLAINS looks at the phone plaintively after hanging
up. Musical phone sequence stopping for MISS WEST COAST.
[**NOTE:** If SHE did not win the GIRLFRIEND AWARD.] Obvi-*

ously nervous, SHE picks it up.)

MISS WEST COAST. Hello please.

FEMALE CALLER #3. (On Tape.) I follow all the fashion tips in the magazines. It takes hours. But I never end up looking like the pictures. What's missing?

MISS WEST COAST. *(Thinks a moment.)* Could you repeat the question?

FEMALE CALLER #3. (On Tape.) What's missing?

MISS WEST COAST. That's why American is the greatest country in the world — because you can get help even on a telephone ... for free.

FEMALE CALLER #3. (On Tape.) What?

MISS WEST COAST. Bye.

[NOTE: If MISS WEST COAST was the winner of the "Girlfriend Award," use the following sequence for MISS INDUSTRIAL NORTHEAST.]

MISS INDUSTRIAL NORTHEAST. *(Obviously nervous.)* Buenos noches.

FEMALE CALLER #3. (On Tape.) I follow all the fashion tips in the magazines. It takes hours. But I never end up looking like the pictures. What's missing?

MISS INDUSTRIAL NORTHEAST. *(Thinks a moment.)* Could you repeat the question?

FEMALE CALLER #3. (On Tape.) What's missing?

MISS INDUSTRIAL NORTHEAST. That's why America is the greatest country in the world — because you can get help even on a telephone... for free.

FEMALE CALLER #3. (On Tape.) What?

MISS INDUSTRIAL NORTHEAST. Bye.

("Musical phones" stops for MISS BIBLE BELT.)

MISS BIBLE BELT. This is Ruth Anne. Praise him!

FEMALE CALLER #4. (On Tape.) *(In tears.)* I have always been ugly. Even plastic surgeons have given up on me. My life is unrelieved misery and pain. I want to die.

MISS BIBLE BELT. First of all, stop your whining and count your blessings, young lady. Be grateful that you have eyes to see how ugly you are. Be thankful that you have ears to hear those plastic surgeons say there is no hope. Get down on your knees and say, "thank you, Jesus" that you are fortunate enough to have a telephone so you can call us and get the help you need. God bless you.

(MISS DEEP SOUTH triumphantly answers the final question.)

MISS DEEP SOUTH. How may I help you?

FEMALE CALLER #5. (On Tape.) What if men had to worry about make-up and parading around in high-heels? Why do we have ridiculous standards of beauty pushed down our throats? Why do we buy this stuff? Why???

MISS DEEP SOUTH. Because we're not men, we're women! And it is our God-given duty to make ourselves beautiful so that the world is a better place and men have something nice to look at while they run it.

FRANKIE. *(Entering.)* I think all of these girls deserve a great big hand!

(MUSIC #24 — "SOMETHING EXTRA" — REPRISE)

(On applause, CONTESTANTS exits.)

FRANKIE. (cont.) Ladies and gentlemen, tonight is only the beginning for Miss Glamouresse [UPCOMING YEAR], but it's the beginning of the end for Miss Glamouresse [CURRENT YEAR]
SHE WAS GREAT
AND SHE WAS SWELL
SHE MADE HER MARK
IN EVERY MALL AND EACH MOTEL
SHE'S A SYMBOL OF ACHIEVEMENT AND SUCCESS
MISS GLAMOURESSE
Ladies and gentlemen, Miss Glamouresse, [CURRENT YEAR], Tawny-Jo Johnson!
SHE'S SOMETHING EXTRA!

(TAWNY-JO is played by the actor who portrayed the winner of the "Girlfriend Award" [either MISS WEST COAST or MISS INDUS-TRIAL NORTHEAST]. SHE is revealed Upstage Center in silhouette and as the lights come up we see SHE has developed quite a full figure. An exuberant good-time gal, TAWNY-JO is wearing the "MISS GLAMOURESSE" banner and crown.)

FRANKIE. Well, Tawny-Jo, it looks like you had quite a year!

TAWNY-JO. Indeed I did, Frankie. I got so much love from all those wonderful people this year. They gave me friendship and testimonial dinners and breakfasts and lunches and buffets. Thanks to them, I discovered the true size of my natural beauty and, Frankie, Bo Derek may be a ten but I'm an eighteen!

FRANKIE. You certainly are, Tawny-Jo. Inspiring — that's what I call it. And I guess the folks at Glamouresse feel the same way. Because tonight, in your honor, they are introducing a brand new product for women just as big and beautiful as you are.

(MUSIC #25 — SPOKESMODEL #7)

TAWNY-JO. That's right, Frankie. And if you'll be so kind as to follow me over to our beauty product launching pad, I'd be happy to demonstrate.

(SHE moves to Spokesmodel area.)

TAWNY-JO. (cont.) Hey, big gals, aren't you tired of those skinny-minny models trying to sell you a teensey bottle of perfume for a great big price? I certainly am. So Glamouresse helped me create a scent for all of us who are large and lovely. Tonight, we are proud to introduce: "Largesse." *(SHE displays an enormous bottle of perfume.)* A lot of scent for a lot of woman. "Largesse" is for the gal whose heart is as big as her waistline. And "Largesse" comes with its own full-size applicator, adjustable to "spray" or "stream." *(SHE demonstrates both.)* Because there's more of you, there's more that needs to be covered with this delicate, yet assertive, fragrance. The bigger you are, the harder you'll fall for "Largesse" from Glamouresse.

FRANKIE. *(Entering.)* Thank you, Tawny-Jo.

(MUSIC #26 — "GOODBYE")

FRANKIE. (cont.) Ladies and gentlemen, as Miss Glamouresse [CURRENT YEAR] enjoys her final moments, the Girls *(Continuing as the CONTESTANTS enter.)* and I have something to say:
BEFORE WE SAY "GOODBYE,"
IT SEEMS TO US
YOU OUGHT TO KNOW JUST WHAT
GOODBYE MEANS TO US

(As FRANKIE sings the letters, HE spells them out in sign language.)

"G"
   CONTESTANTS.
MEANS GEE, IT'S TIME FOR YOU TO GO
   FRANKIE.
"O"
   MISS BIBLE BELT.
MEANS ONLY PAIN CAN MAKE YOU GROW
   FRANKIE.
"O" AGAIN
   MISS BIBLE BELT.
MEANS ONLY IN SORROW
WILL YOU FIND THE COURAGE
TO MAKE IT THROUGH TOMORROW
   FRANKIE.
"D"
   MISS DEEP SOUTH.
MEANS DEPRESSION IS EXPECTED
ESPECIALLY ON THE DAY
WHEN YOUR SUCCESSOR IS ELECTED
   FRANKIE.
"B"
   MISS GREAT PLAINS.
MEANS BE CHEERFUL

FRANKIE.

"Y"

MISS WEST COAST.

MEANS WHY BE SAD AND GLUM AND TEARFUL

FRANKIE.

"E"

MISS TEXAS.

MEANS EVEN THE MOST BEAUTIFUL FLOWER MUST

ALL.

DIE

GOODBYE,

FRANKIE.

OLD QUEEN,

ALL.

GOODBYE

FRANKIE. Tawny-Jo Johnson will now distribute score cards to our judges. But before she does, she will demonstrate the proper way for you judges to display your score. Tawny-Jo.

TAWNY-JO. Now, judges, when judging hold up one card at a time. Just one. So we can see both sides. One side for Frankie and one side for the audience. Like this. And hold it high above your head. Like this. Now, Judges, if you'll just raise your hands... like this... I'll give you your cards. *(FRANKIE hands judges' cards to TAWNY-JO.)* Thank you, Frankie.

FRANKIE. Judges, you've seen the girls compete in the following categories: Evening Gown, Talent, Swim-suit, Physical Fitness, Spokesmodel and Beauty-Crisis Call.

(During the following, TAWNY-JO begins miming the rest of FRANKIE's speech — sort of a combination of signing and visual aid enhancement.)

FRANKIE. (cont.) And now as I call out the name of each finalist, will you assign each contestant a single number score between one and ten. Please hold the number high above your head so that the audience and I may clearly see it. I will compute a sum of those scores and Tawny-Jo Johnson will record it for all but the girls to see *(On "but," TAWNY-JO points to her behind, then indicates the "girls".*

and then points to her eyes on "see." CONTESTANTS applaud TAWNY-JO.) Ladies, please.

(MUSIC # 27 — THE FINAL JUDGMENT)

(The CONTESTANTS turn around, revealing individual heart-shaped mirrors attached to their backs, upon which TAWNY-JO will record their scores with a lipstick.)

FRANKIE. (cont.) All right, Judges, I wouldn't want to be in your shoes. May we have your scores for our first finalist — Miss Bible Belt.

(As the JUDGES vote, TAWNY-JO reminds the audience of each CONTESTANT's talent by miming/singing/speaking throughout the following voting procedure: the CONTESTANT holds up her hand when FRANKIE asks the JUDGES for her votes, the JUDGES hold up score cards, Olympic style. FRANKIE computes the sum of the judges' actual votes on a clipboard with the help of an attached pocket calculator and secretly shares the result with TAWNY-JO. SHE, in turn, writes the result with lipstick on the mirror of the CONTESTANT — in this case, MISS BIBLE BELT.)

TAWNY-JO.
BANKING ON JESUS
OH WHAT A FRIEND
THE BIBLE'S MY BANK BOOK
HUMBLY I SPEND

FRANKIE. Okay, Judges, your scores for Miss West Coast.
[OR] Miss Industrial Northeast
[whichever didn't win the "Girlfriend Award"]

(Same action.)

TAWNY JO. I am born. *(SHE screams.)* [OR, in the case of MISS INDUSTRIAL NORTHEAST *SHE mimes skating and accordion playing.]*

FRANKIE. And if we may have your scores for finalist number three — Miss Deep South.

(Same action.)

TAWNY-JO.
CAMPTOWN LADIES SING THIS SONG
DOO DAH, DOO DAH
CAMPTOWN RACETRACK FIVE MILES LONG
OH DEE DOO DAH DAY!
    How does she do that?
    FRANKIE. And let's tally up Miss Texas.

(Same action.)

TAWNY-JO.
THERE'S A YELLOW ROSE IN TEXAS!
(Miming shooting.) Bang!
    FRANKIE. And finally, your vote for Miss Great Plains.

(Same action.)

TAWNY-JO.
    I am the Land. Shhh! Listen!
(TAWNY-JO records the score on MISS GREAT PLAINS' mirror, touches up her own lipstick in the mirror and then addresses audience.) Audience, let's have a round of applause for our judges. Weren't they wonderful?
    FRANKIE. Thank you, ladies, will you turn around please.

(MUSIC #28 — "TURN AROUND PLEASE")

    FRANKIE. (cont.) It's time to make a little history. *(Drum roll.)* Second runner-up and winner of twelve pairs of full-fashion hosiery, Miss _____ *(SECOND RUNNER-UP crosses to TAWNY-JO and receives a kiss.)* First runner-up and winner of a complete Glamouresse make-over, Miss_____ *(FIRST RUNNER-UP proceeds as SECOND RUNNER-UP did.)*

*[**PLEASE NOTE:** It is not inappropriate for one of either Miss Texas or Miss Bible Belt to be a sore loser and pout, glare at the judges and sulk through the final number, making her hard feelings very evident throughout the rest of the show. But ONE only, please. If MISS TEXAS is First or Second Runner-up or doesn't place, SHE should become the sore loser immediately. MISS BIBLE BELT becomes the sore loser only if MISS TEXAS wins MISS GLAMOURESSE]*

FRANKIE. (cont.) And now the moment we've all been waiting for... *(The remaining THREE FINALISTS huddle together holding hands)* Miss Glamouresse [UPCOMING YEAR] — Miss _____ _____!!!

*([**NOTE:** In case of a tie, FRANKIE will instruct the audience to register their vote by applause. TAWNY-JO will indicate, by miming her, which CONTESTANT is being judged and FRANKIE will make the final decision] The WINNER screams, then perhaps cries. The TWO LOSERS kiss and congratulate WINNER — ONE standing directly in front of her. The other LOSER pushes her out of the way so WINNER can cross to FRANKIE. As FRANKIE sings, TAWNY-JO removes mirror from WINNER'S back, takes off her "Miss Glamouresse" banner and places it on WINNER, gives WINNER a rose bouquet, removes crown from her own head and crowns WINNER.)*

FRANKIE. (cont.) Look at her!

(MUSIC #29 — "MISS GLAMOURESSE")

FRANKIE. (cont.) Isn't she beautiful? And, of course, we know what she's thinking right now:
LOOK AT YOU
THIS MORNING YOU WERE LOST IN THE CROWD
YOU WERE THE ONE WHO SCRAPED AND BOWED
BUT NOW EV'RYONE IS LOOKING AT YOU —
MISS GLAMOURESSE!
    Take a walk!

(During the following the new MISS GLAMOURESSE parades down the runway waving and crying.)

FRANKIE. (cont.)
MISS GLAMOURESSE
THE QUEEN OF LOVELINESS!
BOTH IN AND OUT OF YOUR DRESS
THE JUDGES SAID, "OH YES!"

WITH A TALL AMERICAN
ALL-AMERICAN DREAM
YOU TOOK A SIMPLE NOTION
LIKE SELF-PROMOTION
AND PUSHED IT TO THE EXTREME

MISS GLAMOURESSE
THE QUEEN OF LOVELINESS!
MAY AMERICA BLESS
MISS GLAMOURESSE!

(MISS GLAMOURESSE reads from a scroll which TAWNY-JO hands her.)

MISS GLAMOURESSE.
I wish that you may know in your life
The prettiness I've known in mine
For each of us can do our part
To make the world more beautiful
And what better place to make a start
Than on your face or in your heart
True Beauty's found beneath your dress
And Beauty lives at Glamouresse

(MUSIC #30 — "SHE'S THE ONE!")

CONTESTANTS.
OOO OOO OOO AHH
MISS GLAMOURESSE

SHE'S THE ONE
   FRANKIE.
SHE'S THE ONE
YOU CHOSE TO BE YOUR OWN
   CONTESTANTS.
BE YOUR OWN
   FRANKIE.
SHE'S THE ONE
   CONTESTANTS.
IT'S YOU!
   FRANKIE.
IT'S YOU AND YOU ALONE
SHE'S THE ONE
WHEN ALL IS SAID AND DONE
SOMEONE HAD TO WIN YOUR LOVE AND
   FRANKIE.

SHE'S THE ONE!	**CONTESTANTS.**
	SHE'S THE ONE!
SHE'S THE ONE!	
	SHE'S THE ONE!
SHE'S THE ONE!	
	SHE'S THE ONE!
SHE'S THE ONE!	
	SHE'S THE ONE!

   FRANKIE.
YOUR LIFE WAS FINE
YOU HAD IT WELL IN HAND
NOTHING EXCITING
OR SPECTACULAR PLANNED
   CONTESTANTS.
YOU WERE PART OF A TEAM
ALWAYS ON THE RUN
   FRANKIE AND CONTESTANTS.
BUT YOU STOOD OUT FROM THE REST
NOW

FRANKIE.
SHE'S THE ONE!

SHE'S THE ONE!

SHE'S THE ONE!

SHE'S THE ONE!

CONTESTANTS.
SHE'S THE ONE!

SHE'S THE ONE!

SHE'S THE ONE!

SHE'S THE ONE!
MISS GLAMOURESSE

(Upstage an elaborate vanity, overflowing with make-up and other gifts — luggage, hair-dryer, etc., is revealed. MISS GLAMOUR-ESSE screams and runs to it.)

CONTESTANTS AND FRANKIE.
GLAMOURESSE
HAS GOT A BRAND NEW QUEEN
NOTHING LESS
THAN BEST WE'VE EVER SEEN

(The CONTESTANTS swarm around MISS GLAMOURESSE at her vanity. The designated SORE LOSER picks up a can of hairspray and lets the WINNER have it.)

FRANKIE.
SHE'S THE ONE
WHEN ALL IS SAID AND DONE
FRANKIE AND CONTESTANTS.
HERE'S A SHOW OF THANKFULNESS
FROM GLAMOURESSE
   FRANKIE. *(Over the following.)* Thank you ladies and gentle-men, you've been beautiful. Stay that way. And remember, beauty lives at "Glamouresse!"
   CONTESTANTS.
GLAMOURESSE
GLAMOURESSE

GLAMOURESSE
GLAMOURESSE

*(THEY start coming Downstage for bows in the following order —
   TAWNY-JO, MISS GREAT PLAINS, MISS DEEP SOUTH, MISS
   WEST COAST, MISS BIBLE BELT, MISS TEXAS and FRANKIE.)*

CONTESTANTS AND FRANKIE. *(To the audience.)*
LOOK YOUR BEST
DON'T ASK WHY
JUST BUY
BYE
BYE

(MUSIC #31 — EXIT)

CURTAIN

END OF PLAY

PROP LIST

SPOKESMODEL SPOTS

MISS TEXAS
        LipSnack Demo
        LipSnack Display
MISS GREAT PLAINS
        Hair Aware Hairspray
        Hair Aware Mask
MISS WEST COAST
        Snappin' Fresh Bands
        Snappin' Fresh Display Stand
MISS INDUSTRIAL NORTHEAST
        Solar Rollers and Wig
        Eggroll
        Solar Rollers Scarf
MISS DEEP SOUTH
        Puff 'n' vac w/Compact
        Puff 'n' vac Bib
MISS BIBLE BELT
        Facial Spackle Jar & Bucket
        Spackle Knife
        Pitted Plywood & Stand
TAWNY-JO JOHNSON
        Largesse

TALENT COMPETITION

MISS DEEP SOUTH
        Grandma Jeanie Puppet
        Col. Summerford Puppet
        Stool (placed by FRANKIE)
MISS BIBLE BELT
        Melody Bells on Table with Cover for them
MISS TEXAS
        Hobby Horse

      Lasso
      Holster
      Guns & Caps
MISS INDUSTRIAL NORTHEAST
        Accordion
        Roller Skates

OTHER

FRANKIE CAVALIER
        6 Towels (for "Girl Power")
        Girlfriend Award
        Clipboard & Calculator
        Pencil
TAWNY-JO JOHNSON
        Judges' Score Cards
        Lipstick for Scores
        Miss Glamouresse Scroll
        Crown and Sash
        Bouquet

Glove & Envelope (Announcement of finalists)
Beauty Crisis Phone
Contestant Heart Mirrors (on their backs, for scoring)
Vanity with Chair for Miss Glamouresse
        Vanity Products
        Winner's Hairspray

COSTUME LIST

COSTUMES COMMON TO ALL CONTESTANTS

2 Smocks for Spokesmodel — Shared by ALL (One Stage Left, One Stage Right)

"NATURAL BORN FEMALES and "Crisis Calls"
  6 blue Tea Dresses with title Banners
  6 Pairs of white 3-inch heel Character Shoes
  6 Pairs of short white Gloves (for Opening only)

"IT'S GOTTA BE VENUS"
  6 white spandex Swim-suits with pink title Banners
  6 gold "Space Capes" (worn over Swim-suits)
  Same white Character Shoes as above
  Pink head Towels

INDIVIDUAL CHARACTERS

MISS BIBLE BELT
  Blue silk and beaded Evening Gown
    Matching satin high Heels, long Gloves
  Maroon velvet Palazzo Pants & Bustier for Talent
    Black Heels
    Matching rhinestones with both outfits

MISS DEEP SOUTH
  Blue tulle cotillion Evening Gown — (worn with
    Character Shoes)
  White & green floor length chintz Talent Costume
    (2 piece) with white Pantaloons (Scarlett O'Hara)
    (Character shoes) (Matching necklace & earrings).

MISS GREAT PLAINS

Beige Evening Gown with daisy Headdress & daisies
on skirt
Small rhinestone Earrings, short Gloves Beige
satin Pumps
Green, knee-length Overalls for talent;
Matching Shirt, pocket Kerchief Vegetable Pin &
straw Hat covered with vegetables
Black patent high Heels with ankle Socks

MISS INDUSTRIAL NORTHEAST

Brightly colored, strapless & gathered Evening Gown,
long gloves
Matching bright bangle Earrings & Bracelet
Matching ankle-strapped Heels
Brightly colored, Spanish-style Talent Costume — knee
length
Flower Hair Ornament, black lace long open Gloves,
Roller Skates with pom-poms

MISS TEXAS

Gold strapless brocade-like Evening Gown with fur trim
Matching, large rhinestone Earrings & Necklace;
Fur-trimmed long Gloves, matching satin high Heels
Red, white & blue sequined Talent Costume
(singlet)
Cowboy Hat with rhinestones, rhinestone Earrings,
long blue Gloves, gold jingle Tap Shoes

MISS WEST COAST

Tie-dyed, brightly colored Evening Gown with long Gloves,
Necklace with large crystal, matching Earrings, Hair
Ornament, matching colored ankle-strap Heels
Tie-dyed Unitard with small ballet skirt attached; spandex
Graham-like "Body Bag"; white flat ballet Shoes

FRANKIE CAVALIER
    Opening until "Venus":
        Purple Jacket with rhinestone accents; black Pants,
            white Shirt, black patent Shoes, tacky Jewelry
    "Venus":
        Gold Space Suit with Head Piece (Antennae);
            gold boots
    After "Venus" through end:
        Grey tails with rhinestone accents; white tux Shirt with
            rhinestone studs; black patent Shoes.

TAWNY-JO JOHNSON
    Pink beaded sheath gown with matching ostrich boa
        trim on collar, sleeves and hem (nude padding for
        tummy, hips and bust), crystal drop Earrings, pink
        satin 3" Pumps with stiletto heel
    Large rhinestone Tiara and pink ribbon "Miss Glamouresse"
        Banner (which are passed over to Pageant WINNER.)